5/6 an £1·00

The Depository
A dream book

ANDRZEJ
KLIMOWSKI

faber and faber

First published in 1994
by Faber and Faber Limited
3 Queen Square London WC1N 3AU

Printed in England by Clays Ltd, St Ives plc

A CIP record for this book
is available from the British Library

ISBN 0-571-17286-5

2 4 6 8 10 9 7 5 3 1

for
Danusia
Dominik
and
Natalia

[redacted]

23]

33]

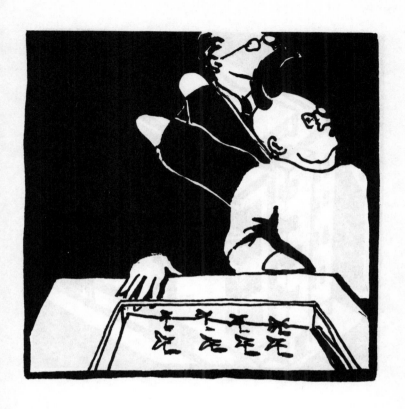

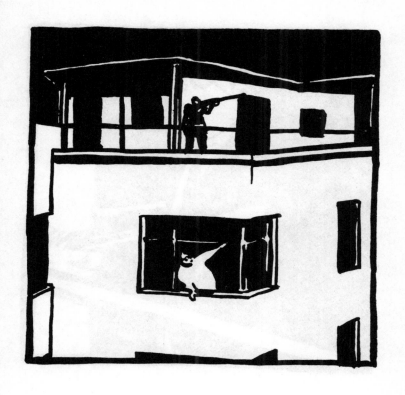

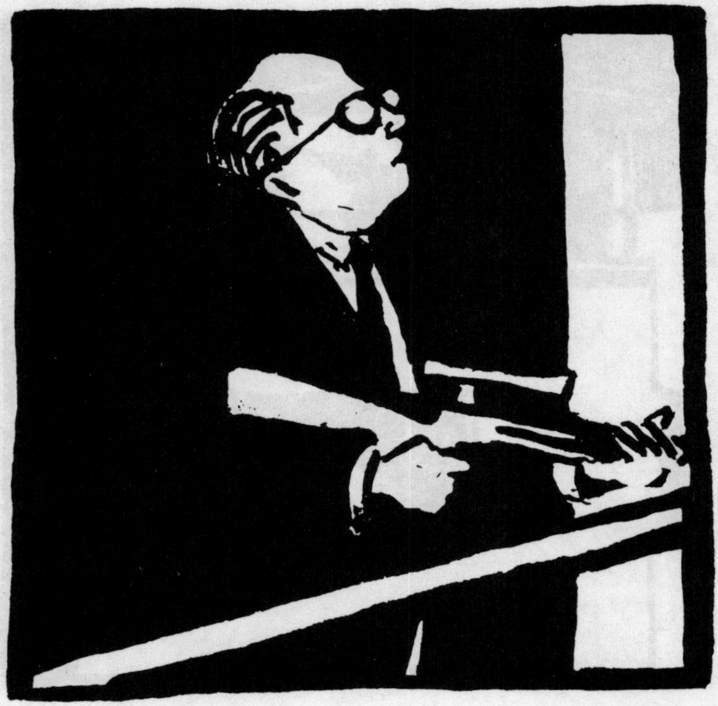
NP

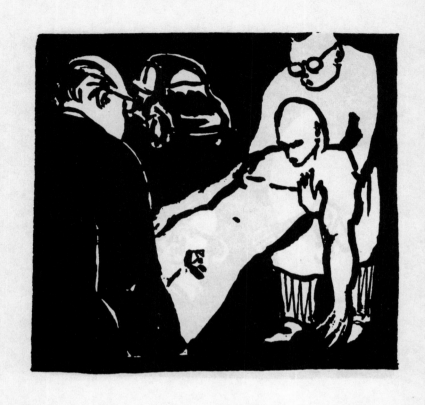

73]

81]

89]

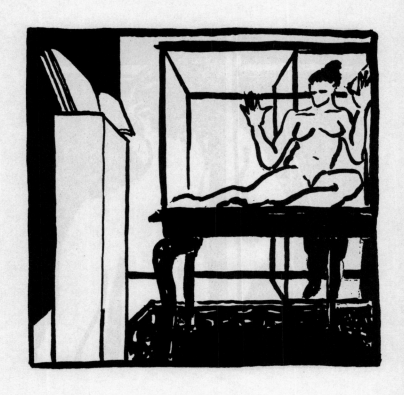

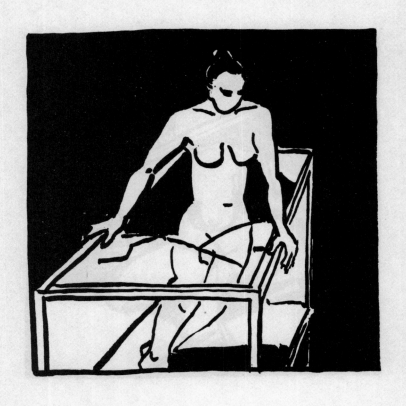

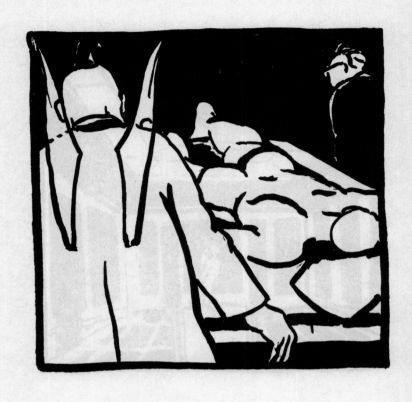

215]

De Memoria et Reminiscentia

235]

243]